AT THE AUTO REPAIR CENTER

Written by Justine Korman

Illustrated by Steven James Petruccio

SCHOLASTIC INC.

New York   Toronto   London   Auckland   Sydney

ISBN 0-439-04286-0

12 11 10 9 8 7 6 5 4 3 2   0/0 01 02 03 04

Printed in the U.S.A.   24
First printing, May 1999

One morning Drew's day care provider was sick.
"My schedule is completely full today. How about yours?" his mom asked.
His dad said, "He can come to work with me at the shop."
Drew cheered. "I'm going to be a mechanic!"

Soon, Drew and his dad arrived at the auto repair center. Jack introduced his son to the receptionist. "Julie makes appointments for all the people who need their cars fixed," he explained.

Jack took Drew inside the shop
to meet the other mechanics.
They all wore overalls like Drew's dad.
Repairing cars and trucks is grimy work!

Julie's voice came over the loudspeaker. "Mr. Grant is here for his tune-up."
Jack drove the limousine into the shop. "Mr. Grant is a professional driver," he told Drew. "We work together to keep his limo in top shape."

First, Drew watched his father change the limo's air filter.
"Cars have lots of filters to keep them clean," Jack explained.

Jack also checked other filters, like the oil filter,
the transmission filter, and the fuel filter. He replaced
the dirty filters with clean ones.

"Now let's check the oil. Oil keeps a car's parts running smoothly," Jack said. He showed his son how to use the dipstick.

"First wipe it clean. Then put it back in the hole and take the stick out again. See the marks?" Jack asked. Drew saw two lines. One was marked FULL, the other ADD. Shiny, brown oil came up to just under the FULL mark.

"Mr. Grant doesn't need oil today," Jack said.

Julie's voice came over the loudspeaker. "Jack, we need an emergency tire change." Mrs. Hamilton's station wagon had blown a tire just in front of the auto repair center! Jack asked if she wanted him to check the other tires to see if they were worn out, too.
"Yes, please!" Mrs. Hamilton exclaimed.

"I've also been hearing a funny squeal,"
Mrs. Hamilton added. "And a strange rattle."
Jack nodded. "I'll check into those, too."
In the shop, Jack said to his son, "Cars can't tell
us what's wrong with them. But sights, sounds,
and even smells are clues to trouble. Lots of things
might be causing the car's noises. We'll play detective
and find out what! But first, we'll change that flat tire."

The hydraulic jack lifted the station wagon off the shop's
cement floor. Jack used a lug wrench to loosen the big
nuts holding the flat tire to the wheel.

After he changed the tire, Jack checked the other tires
for wear. All of them were too old to be safe. Instead of
having deep grooves for gripping the road, they were
flat and smooth. So, Jack changed those tires, too.

Now Jack was ready to listen to the car's noises. "The squeal might be caused by a loose drive belt," Jack said. He lifted the wagon's hood to check the drive belt. The belt was not frayed or hanging loose.

"Let's check the brakes," he said. Jack examined the brake shoes that stop the tires from spinning when the driver wants the car to stop. "That's the problem. These are as worn out as the tires! We'll have to replace them."

"Lots of things can cause a rattle," Jack said. "Sometimes a window crank is loose or there are pebbles in one of the hubcaps."
Drew opened the glove compartment and saw a baby's rattle.
Jack laughed. "I guess that mystery is solved!"

Jack went into the waiting room to give
Mrs. Hamilton the news. "Thank you!
We'll wait here while you replace the
brake shoes," she exclaimed. "I certainly
don't want to be driving around without
safe brakes."

Soon it was time for lunch. Jack bought drinks
from a lunch truck. "Your truck is sounding
awfully loud today," he observed.
The driver nodded. "It's been that way ever since
I hit a pothole yesterday."
Jack bent down to look under the lunch truck.
"Looks like you've got a hole in your muffler."
The driver said, "Thanks. I'll make an
appointment to get it fixed soon."

After lunch, Jack talked to a young man
named Steve whose used van kept overheating.
"My dad says I bought a lemon," Steve said.
"But I think it's a good van."
Jack said, "We'll see! There are lots of different
reasons for a car to overheat."

"Stand back!" Jack warned. "A hot radiator can build up steam!"
Jack used a heavy rag to protect his hand. Then he slowly turned the radiator cap to release the pressure. WHOOSH! Steam hissed out of the van's radiator.

When the hissing stopped, Jack checked for holes in the radiator and the hoses connected to it. Jack pointed to white streaks on the radiator hoses. "Those streaks mean leaks!" he said.

Jack replaced the worn radiator hoses. Then he said, "Let's check the other hoses." Drew looked at the hoses and tubes that snaked around the van's engine. He pointed to a white powder around the battery caps. "Is that supposed to be there?" he asked.

Jack smiled. "You'll make a fine mechanic! That white powder is corrosion on the battery. We need to clean that off and check the battery."
Jack also checked the van's spark plugs, shocks, belts, filters, and many other parts.

Finally, Jack went back to the waiting room to talk to Steve. "Your van is not a lemon. But it does need a lot of work."

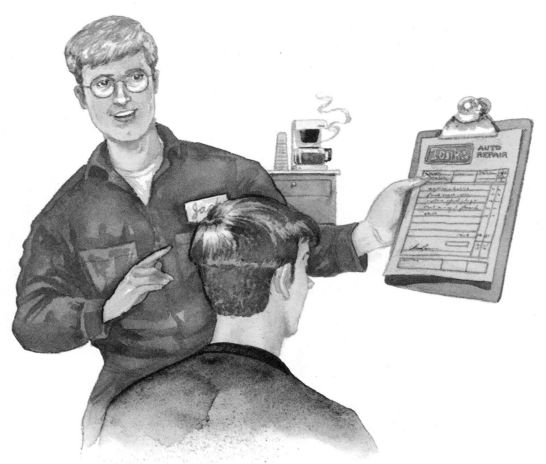

Jack explained everything he would need to do to get the van in tip-top shape. Then he gave Steve an estimate. The estimate included how long Jack thought the work would take as well as how much the replacement parts would cost.
Steve said, "I'll make an appointment right now!"

Jack's next "patient" was Mr. Hatch's off-road vehicle.
"Sometimes the steering pulls," Mr. Hatch explained.
Jack asked, "Do you drive on a lot of rough roads?"
Mr. Hatch chuckled. "All the time! That's why I have
this vehicle."
Jack told Drew, "Going over bumps and potholes can
loosen the connections between the steering wheel and
the power steering mechanism. But, it can be fixed."

"Let's check the suspension sytem," Jack said. "Going over bumps can affect that, too. The suspension system has springs and shock absorbers to cushion a car's ride. When I push down on the front end, the car should only bounce once," he added. Jack pushed down. Drew felt the hood bounce three times!

Jack said, "We'll need to replace the shocks, too."

Next, Jack checked the windshield wipers. "Drivers need to see where they're going," he explained. "Worn out blades won't clear mud off the windshield, and off-road vehicles often drive in mud."
The wipers' metal frames were fine. But Jack replaced the rubber blades because they were warped and cracked.

Jack also checked the washer fluid. "You can help me refill it," he said. Drew held a funnel while Jack poured the blue washer fluid into its container under the hood.

Jack's next appointment was late. While he waited, Jack cleaned up his area. He put away his tools so they would be ready the next time he needed them. Good mechanics don't waste time looking for lost tools.

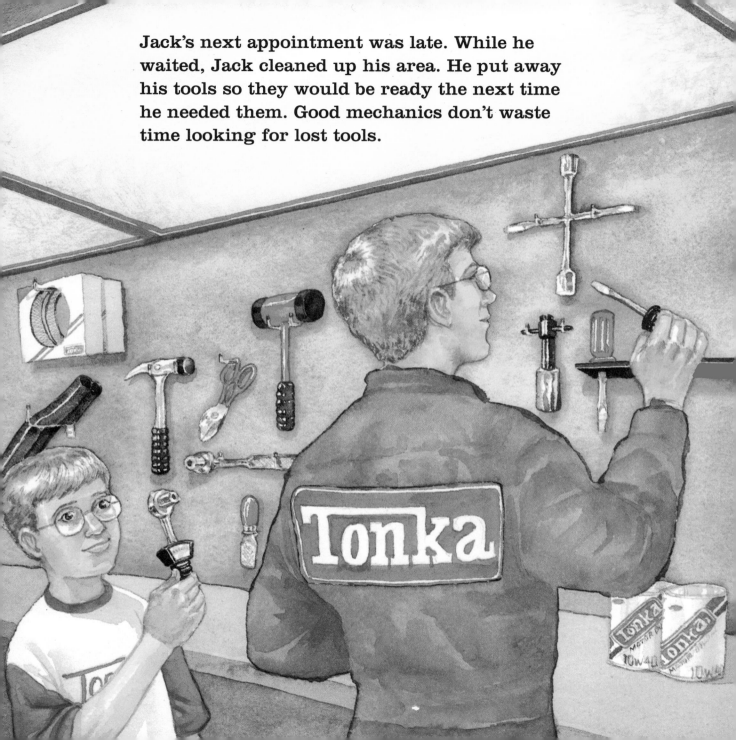

When that was done, Jack read the latest issue of *Modern Mechanics* magazine. Keeping up with new technology is part of a mechanic's job.
"I wonder what cars will be like when you grow up," Jack said.

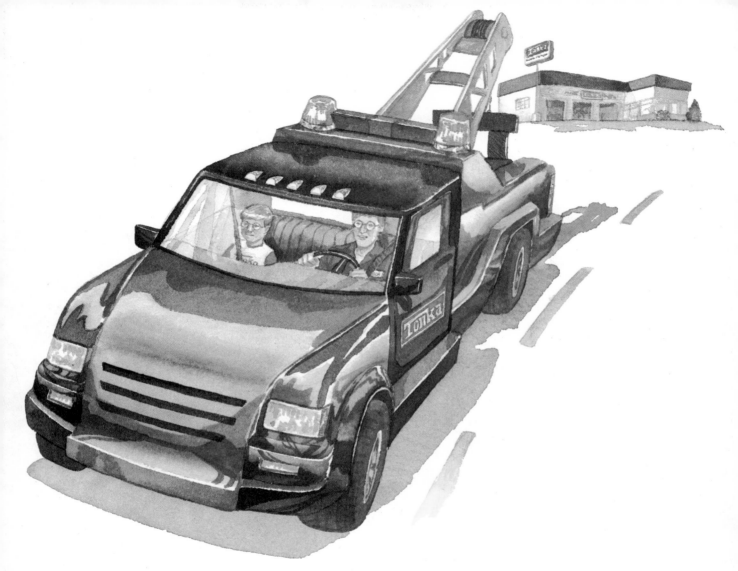

Julie's voice crackled over the loudspeaker. "There's a damaged motorcycle on the highway. Jack, can you pick it up?"
Jack took Drew with him in the tow truck. The powerful truck had a winch in the back to lift the front end of a disabled vehicle off the ground.

Jack said, "A tow truck is like an ambulance for vehicles. It carries them to the shop when they can't make it on their own."

Jack talked to the policeman on the scene.

A car had hit a motorcycle. A real ambulance had already taken the driver to the hospital. He had a broken arm. Jack shook his head. "Safe cars are not enough. People have to be safe drivers, too!"

Jack towed the motorcycle back to the shop. All the mechanics gathered around.

"It wouldn't take much to hammer out that fender," one observed.

"We could salvage the parts," another said.

"But the engine..." Jack bent to get a closer look.

"...The damage might not be as bad as it looks. I bet we can save this motorcycle!"

Drew fell asleep to the sound of hammers, sanders, and drills. Being a mechanic is fun, but it is tiring work!

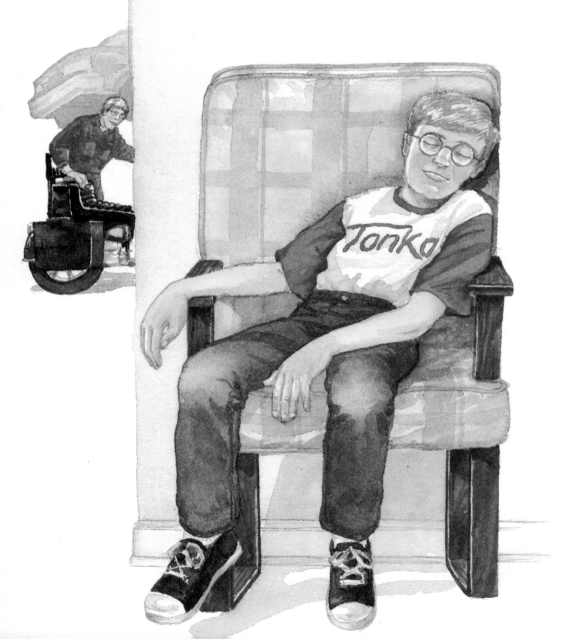